Madeline Valentine

The BAD BIRTHDAY IDEA

Alfred A. Knopf   New York

All Ben ever wanted to do was play with his toy robot . . .

not with his sister, Alice. She liked to play with dolls.

When Alice tried to play with her brother, Ben would say,
"No dolls allowed. This is a robot game."

So Alice told their mom and dad she wanted
the new Roboy 2000 for her birthday.

Ben could not believe his ears.

He really wanted the Roboy 2000. But Mom and Dad
told Ben it was Alice's birthday, not his.

On the day of Alice's birthday party, Ben had to put the wrapped Roboy 2000 on the presents table.

It was so unfair.

That's when Ben had an idea.

He very quietly opened
the wrapping paper.

Then he very carefully opened
the cardboard box and
untwisted the little wires.

"Awesome!" Ben said.

But something terrible happened.

Roboy 2000 crashed into the wall and fell on the floor.

That's when the doorbell rang.

Ben had to find a place to hide the Roboy 2000. Quickly!

He threw the broken robot into the chest.
The wrapping paper and the cardboard box too.

Just then, Alice, Mom, Dad, and all
the guests came into the room.

Alice's friends wished her a happy birthday.
They had snacks and drank punch.

But Ben was not having a good time.

Mom put on music, and everyone started dancing.

Then they played games.

But all Ben could think about was the broken robot.

After everyone had cake and ice cream, Alice opened the gifts
from all her friends. But there seemed to be one missing.

"Where is the family's gift?" Dad asked.
"Go get it, please, Ben," said Mom.

Ben got up from the table.

He walked very slowly to the chest.

He opened it.

Everyone gasped. One kid screamed.
"Oh, Ben!" Mom cried. Alice just stared.

"I am so, so sorry,"
Ben said quietly.

He felt horrible. He had
ruined Alice's birthday.

But he had an idea that he hoped
would make his sister feel better.

Ben went to his room
and found his own
favorite robot.

He held it out to Alice.
"I want you to have
this," he told her.

"Thank you," said Alice. "Will
you play with me now, Ben?"

"Yes, I would love to," said Ben.

To Katie,
for all the weird things we did as kids

THIS IS A BORZOI BOOK PUBLISHED BY ALFRED A. KNOPF

Copyright © 2013 by Madeline Valentine
All rights reserved. Published in the United States by Alfred A. Knopf, an imprint of Random House Children's Books,
a division of Random House, Inc., New York.
Knopf, Borzoi Books, and the colophon are registered trademarks of Random House, Inc.
Visit us on the Web! randomhouse.com/kids
Educators and librarians, for a variety of teaching tools, visit us at RHTeachersLibrarians.com
Library of Congress Cataloging-in-Publication Data
Valentine, Madeline.
The bad birthday idea / by Madeline Valentine.
p. cm.
Summary: Ben refuses to play with his sister, Alice, because he likes robots and she likes dolls, but when her birthday wish
is for a robot that Ben really wants, he opens it first, accidentally breaks it, then tries to cover up his deed.
ISBN 978-0-449-81331-7 (trade) — ISBN 978-0-449-81332-4 (lib. bdg.) — ISBN 978-0-449-81333-1 (ebook)
[1. Brothers and sisters—Fiction. 2. Behavior—Fiction. 3. Birthdays—Fiction. 4. Toys—Fiction. 5. Robots—Fiction.] I. Title.
PZ7.V25214Bad 2013 [E]—dc23 2012042634

The illustrations in this book were created using graphite, gouache, and colored pencils on watercolor paper.
MANUFACTURED IN CHINA
November 2013 10 9 8 7 6 5 4 3 2 1 First Edition